Uncle Pirate

Uncle Pirate

by **Douglas Rees** ⚓ Illustrated by **Tony Auth**

Margaret K. McElderry Books
New York London Toronto Sydney

Margaret K. McElderry Books
An imprint of Simon & Schuster Children's Publishing Division
1230 Avenue of the Americas, New York, New York 10020

Book design by Krista Vossen
The text for this book is set in Edlund.
The illustrations for this book are rendered in pen and ink and watercolor.
Manufactured in the United States of America
2 4 6 8 10 9 7 5 3 1
Library of Congress Cataloging-in-Publication Data
Rees, Douglas.
Uncle Pirate / Douglas Rees ; illustrated by Tony Auth.—1st ed.
p. cm.
Summary: Wilson is one of the most bullied fourth-graders at the chaotic Very Elementary School until his long-lost uncle, Desperate Evil Wicked Bob—a pirate—and his talking penguin arrive and begin making everything ship-shape, one classroom at a time.
ISBN-13: 978-1-4169-4762-2 (hardcover)
ISBN-10: 1-4169-4762-0 (hardcover)
[1. Pirates—Fiction. 2. Uncles—Fiction. 3. Penguins—Fiction. 4. Schools—Fiction.
5. Humorous stories.] I. Auth, Tony, ill. II. Title.
PZ7.R25475Unc 2008
[Fic]—dc22
2006039003

To Signe, Bill, Rob, Rhiannah and Nicky—
a right good crew

—D. R.

For Reese Palley

—T. A.

Uncle Pirate

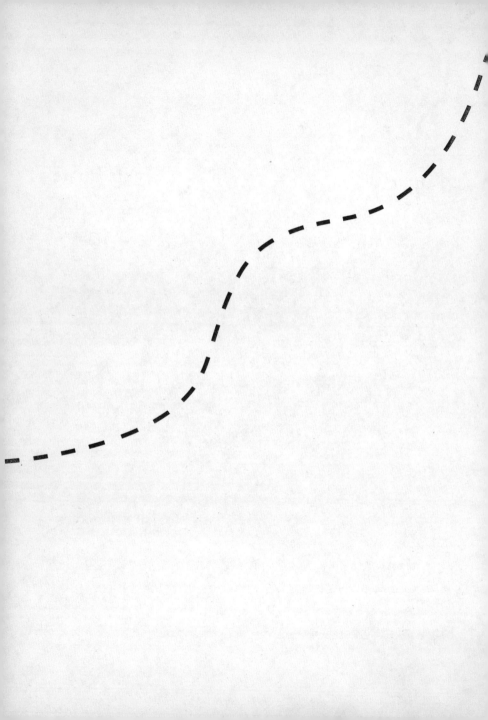

Bad News Pie

There was pumpkin pie for dessert that night. My mom makes the best pumpkin pie in the world. Whenever she does it, I get worried because she only makes it when there's bad news. Dad and I call it Bad News Pie.

I was worried even though her bad news might be good news for me. I'd gotten in another fight at school and my glasses were broken again. I have more pairs of broken glasses than any other kid in the history of fourth grade. There is something about being named Wilson, and being small, and wearing glasses, that makes kids with names like Scott or Jason think they can beat you up. They are usually right.

My parents have to spend a lot of money on glasses. This is bad because we do not have a lot of money.

Maybe a Bad News Pie meant that no one would notice my glasses were broken until after they'd heard

about the thing that made Mom bake the pie. Then a pair of broken glasses might not seem so bad.

But I was still worried.

As soon as she took the pie out of the oven, Dad said, "Who died?"

And I said, "Uh-oh."

Mom smiled at us with a big, fake smile.

"No one's dead, you sillies," she said. "In fact, some-one's alive. Just look."

She put the pie down in front of us and took a piece of paper off the refrigerator. It was an important-looking letter, printed on special paper. She handed it to Dad.

"From the navy?" Dad said. "We don't know anyone in the navy."

"Just read it out loud so Wilson can hear it," Mom said.

"'Dear Ms. Johnson,'" Dad read, "'We found your brother on an island off Antarctica. He said he'd been marooned there for a long time. He had a fishing pole and a penguin with him. Since we didn't know what to do with him, we are sending him to you. He should be there in a couple of days. Sincerely, the U.S. Navy. PS: We are also sending the penguin.'"

Dad put down the letter.

"I don't think you ever said you had a brother," he said to Mom.

"I sort of forgot," Mom said.

"How could you forget you had a brother?" I asked.

"He was a lot older than I was," Mom said. "And he ran away to sea when I was little."

"This is very strange," I said. "The navy has sent me an uncle."

"Do you have any other forgotten relatives I should know about?" said Dad.

"No," said Mom. "Just the brother."

"Where are we supposed to put him?" Dad asked.

Our condo is very small. You can almost open the refrigerator from the living room. My bedroom is the size of a really big box. There are nice houses around us, but they cost a lot. We can't afford one. We couldn't afford one even if I didn't need so many glasses.

Dad looked at the letter again.

"It's six days old," he said. "The navy said he'd be here in a couple of days. I wonder if he got lost."

Just then there was a knock on the front door.

"I'll get it," we all said at once.

We walked to the door in a little knot.

"I'm the daddy. I'll handle this," Dad said.

He opened the door, and there stood the biggest trick-or-treater I had ever seen. He wore a pirate costume, with a big black hat, a patch over one eye, a peg leg, a long red coat, a cutlass, and two old-fashioned flint-lock pistols in his belt. But this was March and he was no kid. He was a rough, red old man with a beard, and a wooden chest at his feet.

Then I saw

the penguin. It came out from behind him. It was one of those big penguins. It must have been four feet tall.

"Permission to come aboard!" shouted the man.

"Uncle"—I gulped it out—"Uncle . . . Pirate?"

"Aye, aye," he said. "Uncle Pirate I be. Be you me sister Emmy's boy?"

"Aye, aye," I answered.

"Then ye be my nevvy," the pirate said. "What be yer name, Nevvy?"

"Wilson," I said.

"Arh, Nevvy Wilson," he said.

Then he saw Mom.

"Emmy, me darling," the pirate said. "Ye've grown."

"Hello, Bob," Mom said. "It's been a long time."

"Aye, ye were but a little squid when I left home," the pirate said.

He reached out and grabbed Dad's arm.

"And ye be the captain of this here dry dock, or I miss my guess," he said. "Shake hands and splice hearts."

5

He took Dad's hand and shook it up and down hard.

"How be ye called, sir?" the pirate said.

"Well, most people call me Steve, actually," Dad said. It was hard for him to talk because his teeth were knocking together from the shaking.

The penguin hopped past us and into the living room.

"Hey!" I said.

"Captain Jack, come back here!" the pirate said, and pushed past us to catch his bird.

"Ye know better than to come aboard a craft without permission," he said, grabbing the bird in his arms.

"I'm hot," said the penguin.

A talking penguin? I thought.

The pirate took the bird back outside and stood there looking at us.

"Please come in," Dad said. "I don't know about the bird, though."

"Oh, Captain Jack'll be no trouble to ye," the pirate said. "He be a good shipmate, really."

"Thanks very much," the penguin said.

We stood back from the door. The pirate put down his bird and picked up his trunk. He put it on his shoulder and came in.

"This be a fine, tight little craft," the pirate said.

"Do you have a refrigerator?" the bird asked. "He told me you would."

"Yes," Mom said. "In the kitchen."

The penguin waddled into the kitchen and opened the refrigerator with his beak. Then he started throwing things out onto the floor.

"Oh, no," said Mom.

"Stop that!" I said.

"Hey!" said Dad. "Do something about your bird."

The penguin forced himself onto the lowest shelf of the refrigerator and lay there looking out at us.

"Thank you," he said.

"Captain Jack won't need but the one shelf," the pirate said.

"Well, we need all the shelves," Mom said. "It's a small refrigerator."

The pirate walked into the kitchen and looked at what the penguin had thrown on the floor.

"Why, these be mostly soda water and such like," he said. "These be no fit drink for a man, nor a lad, nor a woman, neither. Would ye like old Bob to whip you all up a steaming hot bowl of punch before we sling hammocks? That be a proper drink and will help you all to sleep."

"I might be sleeping now," Dad said. "Is this a nightmare I'm having?"

"I don't think so," I said. "Not if there's a pirate and a talking penguin in it."

The pirate laughed.

"Nightmare! Captain Jack and old Bob be as real as ye are," he said. "Now, be ye all snug and shipshape, Captain Jack?" he asked the penguin.

"I'm not coming out of here until morning, if that's what you mean," Captain Jack said.

"Then, I'll be securing the hatch," the pirate said. He started to close the door of the refrigerator.

"Wait a minute," said the penguin. "I won't be able to breathe."

"Arh. We'll pierce ports for ye," the pirate said.

He took his cutlass and stabbed it into the

refrigerator door until it was full of long, ragged slits.

"Stop, Bob!" Mom said.

"You'll ruin the refrigerator," Dad said.

"If I can't breathe, I'll be ruined," the penguin said. "You can close the door now."

The pirate slammed it.

"Wait another minute," said the penguin. "How do I get out?"

"I'll rig you a proper hatch tomorrow, Captain Jack," the pirate said.

"Wait," I said.

I went to the drawer where we keep string and things, and I got out some twine. I tied one end to the top of the refrigerator handle and passed the other end in through one of the slits.

"Pull on that," I said.

The door opened. We saw the penguin with the string in his mouth.

"Now see if you can pull it shut," I said.

The penguin tugged the string and the refrigerator closed. "Good night," said the bird.

"Nevvy, ye be a right smart shipmate," the pirate said, hitting me on the back. "Now then, where do old Bob sling his hammock?"

"Ah. Well," Dad said.

"There isn't much room . . . ," said Mom.

"With ye, Nevvy. Where else?" the pirate said, grinning at me. "Where be the fo'c'sle on this craft?"

"The . . . the bedrooms are upstairs," I said.

"Arh," said the pirate, and he went up the stairs with his wooden chest.

"Bob," Mom called. "Wouldn't you like some dinner?"

"No, thank ye," Bob said. "It were a long trip from Antarctica. I needs to hit the sack. I'll see ye for breakfast."

We heard the door slam.

"He can't stay," Dad said. "Our condo is too small. And we can't afford to feed him and his bird."

"Of course he can't," Mom agreed. "But we have to think of what to do with him."

"Can we keep the penguin?" I asked.

"No!" Mom and Dad said together.

A Really Bad Pirate

When I went up to my room, the pirate was fast asleep in a hammock hanging over my bed. There was hardly room for me to get under the covers without bumping him. He had a nightcap on his head and his pistols in his hands. I saw that the pistols had little skulls and crossed bones on the hammer. They were neat, and scary.

He was snoring like thunder.

I lay there trying to sleep. The hammock almost brushed my nose. The snoring got louder.

"Uncle Pirate, wake up," I said.

Nothing happened.

"Uncle Pirate, please wake up," I said.

Still nothing happened.

I tried a few more times, but the pirate just snored more. I think my bed was shaking.

When Mom and Dad went to bed, they looked into my

room. Dad tried rocking the hammock. Mom tried saying "Bob, wake up" a few times. But the pirate didn't move.

"I don't know what to do," she said at last. "We can't sleep with this."

Then the penguin came into the room.

"Excuse me," he said. "I'll fix this."

He waddled over to the hammock and pecked good and hard.

"Avast!" the pirate roared. "By Billy Bones and Davy Jones, we'll not be boarded! All hands to battle stations."

He waved his pistols in every direction. He knocked over the lamp by my bed. Then he saw where he was.

"You were snoring," the penguin said. "Stop it."

"Oh. Sorry, Captain Jack," the pirate said.

He turned over on his side.

"Good night again," the penguin said, and went downstairs.

Mom picked up my lamp.

"Good night, dear," she said to me.

Dad closed my door.

I looked up at the hammock swinging just above my nose. I thought it looked more interesting than my own bed.

"Uncle Pirate, would you like to trade?" I asked.

"Me, sleep in a real bed with sheets and pillows and all?" he said.

"Sure," I said.

"Nevvy, I will!" the pirate said. He rolled out of the hammock and dived under the covers with me.

"This be shipshape and Bristol fashion," he said.

"What does that mean?" I asked.

"That means all be right, tight, clean, and bright," he said.

I got out on the other side of my bed and climbed into the hammock.

"This be shipshape and Bristol fashion," I said. "Thanks."

14

It felt almost like I was on an adventure. I'd never had one before, but I thought an adventure with Uncle Pirate could be a very good thing. Especially if Captain Jack came along. But that would be good luck, and I wasn't used to good luck. I started to worry that maybe there was something wrong.

"Uncle Pirate, are you really a pirate?" I said.

"Of course I be," the pirate said. "Did ye ever see anybody dress like this who weren't? I were a captain."

"Were you a bad pirate?"

"I were as bad as I knew how to be," Uncle Pirate said.

"That's great," I said. "Did you have a special name, like Blackbeard?"

"I tried some out," the pirate said. "I tried Black Bob. But the crew said it were only a copycat of Blackbeard. Then I tried Red Bob. But the crew said that made no sense. I tried Green Bob. But the crew said that sounded funny. Finally I tried Desperate Evil Wicked Bob. But the crew said that were too long. So I gave up. But I likes the last one best."

"What was the name of your ship?" I asked.

"Ah. That were the *Hyena of the Seas*," he said. "As fine

a craft as ever cut a wake. A black hull, she had. And red sails. And a big black flag with skull and crossbones. The Jolly Roger."

"How come you have a talking penguin?" I asked.

"Well, there weren't no other company on that island in Antarctica," he said. "Just the one penguin. I kept trying and trying to teach him, and finally he spoke up. Better than a parrot, Captain Jack is."

"Who marooned you?" I asked.

The pirate didn't answer at first. Then he said, "They said I were a bad captain."

He said it in a small, sad voice.

"Who did?" I asked.

"Me crew," the pirate said. "They were madder than tiger sharks."

"Why? What did you do to them?" I asked.

"Nothing," he said. "It were only that we weren't making money. It be hard to be a pirate these days. If ye fires a cannonball at a supertanker, it don't even notice. Call on an aircraft carrier to surrender, and she calls back you are ridiculous. Finally me crew got tired of it. They put me ashore in the coldest spot they could find and sailed away. Mutiny, it was. The worst crime there is at sea."

"So you never buried any treasure," I said.

"Not a brass doubloon," the pirate said sadly.

Poor Uncle Pirate. If he had a treasure, I was sure Mom and Dad would let him stay.

Down in my bed I heard Uncle Pirate clearing his throat. It sounded like he was trying not to cry.

I felt like I had to cheer him up.

"I'll bet you were really a good bad pirate," I said. "I'll bet you were just unlucky."

"Maybe," Uncle Pirate said.

"Anyway, that all be past now. No more sea-doggin' for old Bob." Then he said, "Nevvy? Will ye help me?"

"Sure," I said. "Help you what?"

"I ran away when I were young," he said. "And I were a pirate for years. Then I were marooned a long time. Nevvy, I don't recall much about living ashore. Ye must help me to do things right."

"Okay," I said.

"Thanky, Nevvy," Uncle Pirate said. "That be kind of ye. Well, time to get some shuteye, I reckon."

He went back to sleep. This time he didn't snore.

I liked having a pirate for an uncle. I was sure none of the other kids at school had one. And he had a penguin. That was neat. And best of all, Mom and Dad hadn't noticed my glasses were broken. I wanted to keep Uncle Pirate and Captain Jack. And where would they go if we didn't let them stay? Tomorrow I would think of some idea that would make Mom and Dad change their minds.

Fish Sticks + Thunder Slump

"Uncle Pirate, what would you like to be if you couldn't be a pirate?" I asked the next morning.

We were still in bed.

"I never gave it no thought," Uncle Pirate said. "A pirate were all I ever wanted to be."

"Well, we need to find you a job," I said.

"Arh," Uncle Pirate agreed. "So I can buy fish for Captain Jack."

I didn't add, "And so Mom and Dad will let you stay." Instead I tried to think of all the jobs I knew about. Finally I said, "How about a bus driver?"

"That sounds good," Uncle Pirate said. "But I don't know how to drive."

"You never learned to drive?" I asked.

"I ran away from home too early," Uncle Pirate said. "No one ever taught me."

19

"That won't work, then," I said. "What about a paleontologist?"

"That sounds good too," Uncle Pirate said. "What be it?"

"They dig up dinosaur bones and put them in museums," I said.

"Where be these dinosaurs?" Uncle Pirate asked.

"I don't know," I said. "I guess you just have to find them."

"I doubt I'd be much good," Uncle

Pirate said. "I never could find no buried treasure when I were a pirate."

Then I had an idea that seemed perfect.

"Uncle Pirate, you could be a gardener," I said.

"I could?" he said.

"Sure. We have gardens and lawns all around these condos," I said. "I'll bet you could get a job taking care of them."

"What would I have to do?" Uncle Pirate asked.

"Rake leaves and trim the bushes and cut the lawns. And water everything," I said.

"Nevvy, I will!" Uncle Pirate said. "I'll start today."

"Not so fast," I said. "We'd better ask first."

"Arh!" Uncle Pirate agreed. "We'll go and tell them I'm aboard and waiting for orders."

"Okay," I said. "I'll ask the manager after I come home from school."

"A gardener," Uncle Pirate said. "I'll be a gardener, and Captain Jack will help me."

Mom knocked on my door.

"Wilson, time to get up," she said.

We went down to breakfast.

"Good morning, Bob," Mom said.

"Arh, Emmy," Uncle Pirate said. "Good morning, Steve."

"Arh," Dad said. He was reading his paper and not looking at Uncle Pirate or me.

I went to get the milk.

"Time to get up?" Captain Jack said when I opened the door.

"Stir your lazy bones from that sack and stand to!" Uncle Pirate shouted.

"I'm hungry," Captain Jack said. "Where do you fish?"

"I think we have some fish sticks in the freezer," Mom said.

I found the box and held it out to Captain Jack.

"This is fish?" Captain Jack said.

"Sure," I said. I took out one of the fish sticks and held it up. "It just looks funny, that's all."

22

Captain Jack took the fish stick and gulped it down. "Not much fun to catch," he said.

"Try this," I said.

I tossed the next fish stick up in the air. Captain Jack caught it and ate it.

"That was good," he said. "Do it again."

In a minute he had caught every fish stick in the package.

"Thank you," said Captain Jack.

"My nevvy be smart as a whole school of dolphins," Uncle Pirate said. "Now, what about us swabs?"

"Oh, I have Gummy Grain in the morning," I said. "Mom and Dad just have coffee."

"What be Gummy Grain?" Uncle Pirate asked.

I showed him the box.

He read it slowly, putting his finger under each word. "Gummy Grain. For a fast start each morning. Contains pure sugar, wheat products, and food coloring."

"That's what makes the Gummy Grains different colors," I said. "See? Some of them are pink, some are blue, and the really good ones are green."

"Arh," said Uncle Pirate. He got up and went to the stove.

"This crew needs proper grub," Uncle Pirate said. "My crew would have keelhauled me if I'd fed 'em on Gummy Grain and coffee. Not that there be anything wrong with coffee."

Then he tried Mom's coffee.

"Most coffee, anyway," he said. "Captain Jack, go above and fetch the blue bottle from me trunk."

The penguin went upstairs and was back in a minute with a big blue bottle in his beak.

"Emmy, me dear, this be what your coffee needs," he said. He poured some of the bottle's contents into the coffeepot.

24

Then Uncle Pirate got busy with Mom's pans.

He was making something to eat. I didn't know what it was, but it seemed to use some of everything in the refrigerator.

"I like my coffee the way it is," Mom said. "I've been making it the same way since Steve and I were married. Steve likes it too, don't you, darling?"

"Well . . . ," Dad said.

"You mean you don't like my coffee?" Mom said.

"Captain Jack, fill their cups," Uncle Pirate ordered.

Captain Jack picked up the coffeepot. He poured some more coffee into Mom's and Dad's cups.

Dad took a sip and smiled.

"Not bad," he said.

Mom tried it.

"It is pleasant," she said. "What is it?"

"Just a dollop of Old Capstan," Uncle Pirate said. "Hand me that bottle again, Nevvy. This here breakfast is near ready."

I handed him the bottle, and he poured some over the food. It sizzled and smoked. I think I saw sparks.

"Now, tuck in, you lubbers, and no more Grubby Grits or whatever they be," Uncle Pirate said.

I got four plates.

Uncle Pirate gave us each a big lump of what he'd made.

"I don't like a big breakfast," Dad said.

"This be just a half recipe," Uncle Pirate said. "Tuck in, Steve."

Dad tried it.

"Hm," he said. Then he took another bite.

"What do you call this?" he asked.

"It have a special name," Uncle Pirate said. "Thunder slump."

Mom tried hers.

"It's good," she said. "Where did you learn to make it, Bob?"

"From me ship's cook, Rotten Ralph," Uncle Pirate said. "He were so dirty he smelled like bilges at low tide. But he were a good man with a skillet."

I tried mine. It was sort of like everything good I'd ever tasted.

"Wow," I said.

Uncle Pirate sat down and had his.

When we were all finished, Dad said, "That was good, Bob. Maybe when you go to sea again, you should go as a cook."

"That sounds like a great idea," Mom said.

"I be looking for work ashore," Uncle Pirate said. "Mayhap I'll have something by the end of the day."

"Oh," Dad said. "Well, it usually takes longer than that to get work ashore."

Uncle Pirate put his finger alongside his nose and winked.

"Aye, for some lazy wharf rat who don't know what he's doing," he said.

"Well, this lazy wharf rat had better get to work," Dad said. He stood up.

"And this lazy wharf rat had better get to school," I said.

"When tie you up at dockside again?" Uncle Pirate asked me.

"Huh? You mean when do I get home today?" I said. "About two thirty."

"Five bells on the afternoon watch," Uncle Pirate said. "I'll clap eyes on ye then, Nevvy. Don't be forgetting what we talked about."

"I'll not—I won't," I said.

I got my backpack and headed out the door.

I hadn't gone a block when I heard something behind me. It sounded like two rubber gloves walking fast.

I turned around. There was Captain Jack.

"Where are you going?" I said.

"To school," the penguin said. "He said there'd be school."

"Well, there is, but penguins don't have to go," I said.

"I want to go," Captain Jack said. "I want to learn to read and write. All he ever taught me was how to talk."

"But my school's tough," I said. "There are some really mean kids there. They might beat you up."

"Let them try," Captain Jack said. "I'll peck."

"Besides, you can't just go," I said. "Your parents have to register you and everything."

28

"Your parents can do that, can't they?" Captain Jack said. "Please let me go with you."

His head drooped.

"You can't go today because you're not signed up," I said. "But if you go home now, I'll ask Mom and Dad to take you tomorrow."

"All right. But can I watch while you do your homework?" Captain Jack asked.

"Sure, if I have any," I said.

"Thank you," the penguin said. "I'll go with you tomorrow."

He turned around and went back.

I shook my head. If there was one thing I knew, it was that my school was no place for a penguin.

Carla Canova is Going to Kill You

I walked the rest of the ten blocks to my school, Very Elementary. It's named for Vera Very, the first teacher who went crazy working there.

As soon as I got to the playground, I was hit in the head by a volleyball.

"Get out of the way!" shouted the kid who'd thrown it.

He and his friends galloped past me. It was like being stuck in a herd of buffalo. They stomped my feet and yanked on my backpack so that I spun around in a circle.

After them came a pack of sixth graders. They didn't bother to stomp me. They wanted the kids who'd stolen their ball. But I got knocked over again anyway.

I stood up. Over by the playground equipment some kids were having a push war on the slide. Some of the others were having a sand war in the sandboxes. It was just another day at Very Elementary.

Scott saw me. Scott was the kid who'd broken my glasses yesterday. He was very wide and strong. He usually beat me up two or three times a week. But it wasn't because he didn't like me. He just liked me best when he was pounding on me.

"Hey, Wilson, where's your glasses?" he shouted.

"Where's your brain?" I shouted back. It was all I could think of to say.

"I don't have a brain," Scott shouted. He ran over to the water fountain and held some kid's face in it.

"That's what I thought," I said to myself.

Then I saw Jason. He was the kid who beat me up when Scott was too busy.

"Hey, Wilson, look what I've got," he said.

It was a little pink laptop with a unicorn on it. A Pixi Trix. I'd seen them on TV. They had special video games just for girls. They had names like Fairy Fun and Elf Croquet. Every boy in the world thought that they were sissy. So did a lot of girls.

"Guess who I stole this from?" Jason asked.

"Your little sister?" I guessed.

"Wrong," Jason said. "Carla Canova."

"No way," I said. "Carla Canova is the meanest fourth grader in the last hundred years. She would eat a Pixi Trix before she would play with it."

31

"I took it out of her backpack," Jason said.

I was very happy that Jason had stolen Carla Canova's Pixi Trix. Carla Canova was as big as a fifth grader, which was what she should have been. They'd held her back because she couldn't read much.

Carla Canova was so mean that even the sixth graders were afraid of her. When she fought, she kicked. And anybody she kicked limped for a week. Carla had never done anything mean to me, though. I had never given her any reason. And Carla wasn't like Jason or Scott. She wouldn't beat you up without a reason.

"Carla Canova is going to kill you," I said.

"No, she won't."

"Why not?"

"For two reasons," Jason said. "The first reason is she doesn't know it's gone yet."

Then we heard a horrible noise from the other side of

32

the playground. Everybody stopped fighting for a minute and looked. It had to be Carla finding out her Pixi Trix was gone.

"What's the second reason?" I asked.

I was feeling very, very happy now. Jason was going to be turned into playground pudding in one more minute.

"The second reason is I'm going to tell her you did it," Jason said.

He ran away, waving the Pixi Trix over his head.

"Hey, Carla, I found it! Wilson took it. Here it is," he shouted.

I felt too frightened to move. I just stood there waiting for Carla to come and destroy me.

She came toward me slowly. She had to move slowly because she had Jason's head under her arm, and he was screaming and dragging his feet.

"Did you steal my Pixi Trix?" Carla asked me.

"No, he did," I said.

Carla squeezed Jason tighter.

"Did you steal my Pixi Trix?" she asked.

"No, he did," Jason gasped.

"One of you is lying," Carla said. "I think it's Jason."

"It is, it is," I said.

"But it might be you," Carla said. "So I will beat you both up."

"Oh, no," Jason said.

I didn't say anything. I couldn't talk.

"I will beat Jason up now," she said. "And I will beat you up at recess. Meet me by the monkey bars."

Then she took Jason away.

The bell rang a few minutes later. I went to my classroom. I took a seat near the blackboard. We had assigned seats, but nobody sat where they were supposed to. Most of the time nobody sat at all.

Our teacher, Ms. Twissel, was standing in the corner with her back to the wall.

"Good morning, class," she shouted as we came in.

"No, it isn't," we shouted back. We did it every morning.

I saw Carla come in, and then, last of all, came Jason. He was limping on both legs.

"Let's all say the pledge to the flag," Ms. Twissel said.

We all put our hands up in the air like we were being robbed and shouted,

"We pledge allegiance to the Untied Snakes of America and to all that other stuff we don't understand. Amen."

Ms. Twissel said the whole thing right. She did it every morning.

"Now, class, I wonder if we might do some spelling," Ms. Twissel said.

"No!" all the boys shouted.

"Arithmetic?" Ms. Twissel asked.

"No!" all the girls shouted.

"How about some nice science?" Ms. Twissel asked.

"No!" everyone shouted.

I mean everyone but me was doing these things. I was busy thinking about how Carla was going to turn me into recess roadkill. I kept wondering if there was some way I could escape.

If I could only get sent to the principal's office. If I

could make it that far, I might get sent home. Sometimes kids did.

Ms. Twissel was trying to pass out paper.

"Let's all draw pictures," she said.

We took the paper and started to make paper airplanes out of it.

"Ms. Twissel, I've been bad," I said, waving my hand. "Please send me to the principal's office."

"Well, I don't know," Ms. Twissel said. "I haven't seen you do anything bad this morning. You haven't even made a paper airplane yet."

I tried hard to think of some bad thing I could say I'd done. It would have to be something Ms. Twissel would believe. But that wasn't hard. She believed everything.

"I know what I did, I know what I did," I said. "I put Mighty Glue on all the fire extinguishers. No one will be able to take them off the wall if there's a fire."

"Goodness, that was bad of you," Ms. Twissel said. "All right, Wilson. You may go to the principal's office."

"I helped him," Scott said. "I get to go too."

"I thought of it," Jason said. "Please let me go too."

"Principal Purvis doesn't like it when I send so many students," Ms. Twissel said. "I'd better just send Wilson. He can be punished for all three of you."

"Yay!" I said. I got my lunch box and ran out of the room.

Principal Purvis's office was locked. It always was.

I rang a bell. After a while the curtain on the door window opened an inch.

"What do you want?" said the secretary, Ms. Quern.

"Let me in. I've been bad," I said.

"You're all bad," Ms. Quern said.

"Ms. Twissel says I have to see the principal."

"What will you give me to let you in?" Ms. Quern asked.

"I've got cupcakes in my lunch," I said.

"Let's see," she said.

I opened my lunch box and held up the cupcakes.

"Oh. Chocolate. Good," she said. She unlocked the door and I went in.

Ms. Quern held out her hand. "Cupcakes," she said.

I gave them to her.

"He's in there," she said, and pointed.

37

I went into the principal's office. There was no sign of him.

I walked around his desk and looked under it.

He was curled up down there reading. He always was.

He had a big stack of books beside him. I saw *How to Retire Early*, *Easy Ways to Get Rich*, *Where to Find Buried Treasure*, *Winning Lottery Numbers*, and things like that.

"How are you today, Mr. Purvis?" I said.

"What do you want?" he asked.

"I want you to punish me."

"All right. I'll send you back to your classroom," he said.

"No, no. You have to send me home."

"If I can't go home, you can't go home," Principal Purvis said. "Stick it out like the rest of us."

"Mr. Purvis, if you don't send me home, Carla Canova

is going to turn me into monkey-bar boy chunks," I said.

"Isn't she awful?" Principal Purvis said. "Scares me to death."

He shrugged and turned the page of the book he was reading.

"Mr. Purvis, do you hide under your desk because you're afraid of Carla Canova?" I asked.

"It's a lot of things," Principal Purvis said. "I just feel more comfortable here."

"I'd feel more comfortable not getting beaten up," I said. "Just for today. Please send me home."

"Hmm. How much money have you got?" Principal Purvis asked.

"None," I said.

"Then don't bother me."

"I'll give you my lunch," I said.

"Big deal," Principal Purvis said. "I heard you give Ms. Quern your cupcakes."

"But I've still got a peanut butter and jam sandwich," I said.

"What kind of jam?" Principal Purvis asked.

"Strawberry," I said, and held out my lunch box.

Principal Purvis opened it and took a bite out of my sandwich.

"Excellent," he said. "You can go."

So I ran out the door. In fact, I ran five blocks, just in case Carla might be waiting to pounce on me. Then I started walking.

I knew that Carla was still going to turn me into sandbox surprise. But at least she wouldn't do it today. And tomorrow maybe I could think of some new way to escape her.

I felt good until I got close enough to home to see it. Then I stopped and stared. There was a huge pile of branches and leaves on the street. Uncle Pirate was standing beside it.

Every bush around our condos had been cut down.

Uncle Pirate Gets to Work

"Nevvy, why be ye back so early?" Uncle Pirate said. "The sun be scarcely over the yardarm."

"Uncle Pirate, what did you do?" I asked.

"A spot of gardening," Uncle Pirate said.

"I told you to wait for me," I said. "We have to go see the manager first."

"So ye did," Uncle Pirate agreed. "But, thinks I to meself, 'Bob, what'll that manager think when he sees ye? He'll think, "Here be a pirate and not a gardener."' So I thinks, 'Bob, show the son of a seacook what ye can do.' And I done it."

"You sure did," I said.

Our bushes had been nice and tall. Now our condos looked like they were standing on a pool table with sprinklers.

42

"Where did you get the tools?" I asked. I was afraid that, being a pirate, he'd stolen them.

"Tools? What tool do any pirate need but this?" he asked. He yanked out his cutlass and waved it around. "But those bushes, Nevvy, be tricky. Ye chop a bit on one side, it makes the other side look wrong. So ye chop that side, and the first side looks wrong. I finally had to razee the whole lot to the ground. I reckon they'll grow back all shipshape and Bristol fashion."

"Oh, Uncle Pirate," I said. "We're both in a lot of trouble."

"Trouble?" Uncle Pirate grinned. "Just steer me to it, Nevvy. Where be this trouble?"

"Well, in the first place, nobody's going to like what you did," I said. "Everyone liked those bushes. No one will ever hire you to be a gardener now."

"Arh," Uncle Pirate said. "It were lubberly work anyway. But what be your trouble, Nevvy?"

"Never mind about that now," I said. "We still have to find you a job."

"You're a fine lad to help an old pirate get land legs," Uncle Pirate said. "What'll we try next?"

"Sometimes my dad takes me with him to a coffee place he likes. Last time I was there, I saw a Help Wanted sign. Maybe you could work there."

"I makes good coffee," Uncle Pirate said.

"Let's go see if the sign's still up," I said.

It was.

ARE YOU CHEERFUL?
OUTGOING?
HARDWORKING?
DO YOU LOVE COFFEE?
THEN STIRCROCK'S® COFFEE
HAS A JOB FOR YOU!
APPLY RIGHT NOW.

The manager saw us right away. He seemed like a nice man, but jumpy. Maybe it was all the coffee he drank.

"Hi, I'm Nick Blick," he said. "Can you make coffee?"

"Arh!" Uncle Pirate said.

"That means yes," I said.

"Are you cheerful, outgoing, and hardworking?" Nick Blick asked.

"Arh!" Uncle Pirate said.

"When can you start?" Nick Blick asked.

"As soon as you give the order to drop anchor, Captain," Uncle Pirate said.

"Great. You're hired," Nick Blick said. "Come on, I'll show you how to make our drinks."

He took Uncle Pirate behind the counter.

"Everything at Stircrock's is special," Nick Blick said. "You can't get these drinks anywhere else. Just learn their names and the recipes, and you'll do great."

He started to show Uncle Pirate everything at once.

"This is the Espresso Mess," he said. "And this is the Frozen Frapple. And this is the Triple Fripple."

There were a lot of different drinks. And every drink had its own special cup.

"Stircrock's is the biggest coffee company in the world," Nick Blick said. "We got that way by doing everything the same way every time. So just do everything the same way every time, and everything will be great."

"Arh," Uncle Pirate said.

"Great. Glad to have you," Nick Blick said. "By the way, what's your name?"

"I be Cheerful, Outgoing, Hardworking Bob," said Uncle Pirate.

"See you, Bob," said Nick Blick.

He went into the back of the store. He came out a minute later with a mountain bike.

"Where are you going?" I said.

"Out," Nick Blick said. "I haven't had a day off since they made me be manager. That was two years ago. Nobody wants to work here. Bye."

Uncle Pirate looked around and grinned.

"I be a skipper again," he said.

A lady came into the store.

"I'll have a Double Mocha Choker with whip to go," she said.

"Arh!" Bob said.

He bustled around with the pots for a few minutes. Then he handed the lady a cup.

"What's this?" she said.

"A double what-you-said," Uncle Pirate said.

"No, it isn't," the lady said.

"My mistake," Uncle Pirate said. "I made ye our new drink instead. A Captain Kidd Double Squid. How d'ye like it?"

"It's good," the lady said. "Better than what I ordered. I never liked that other thing much anyway."

"Arh!" Uncle Pirate said.

Pretty soon it was close to lunchtime. Stircrock's started to get busy.

"I'll have a Java Jingle," someone would say. Or, "I'll have a Not a Lot o' Latte."

Every time Uncle Pirate would grin and try to make what they said. Every time they would say it wasn't what they had asked for. Every time Uncle Pirate would say it was a new drink. Every time they would say it was better than what they'd wanted.

Nobody left. They stayed and ordered more drinks. Uncle Pirate gave them Crow's Nest Cappuccinos, Fo'c'sle Froths, and Blackbeard Bitter Blasters.

Customers started calling people on their cell phones. They told their friends to get down to Stircrock's and try the great new drinks. In two hours there was a crowd in front of the store. People were passing money forward and passing coffee back. They were smiling and laughing. They were even toasting each other and saying "Arh!"

I was so proud of my uncle. I wished Mom and Dad and Captain Jack could have been there.

It was getting dark when Nick Blick came back.

At first he looked surprised. Then he looked at all the money, and he hugged Uncle Pirate and danced him around.

Then he looked at the drinks.

He stopped smiling.

"Bob, what are you doing?" he said. "You've made all the drinks wrong."

48

"No, he didn't!" everyone shouted. "He just made them different."

"Different is wrong!" Nick Blick shouted. "This is Stircrock's."

"We want our Caramel Carronades," the customers said. "We want our Triple Topsails."

"You can't have them," Nick Blick shouted. "You have to drink what we make."

"No, we don't," the customers said. "If we can't have what we want, we won't come here."

"But this is Stircrock's," Nick Blick shouted. "Everyone comes here."

"We'll never come here again," they all shouted.

And they all pushed out the doors, still shouting, and throwing their empty cups at Nick Blick.

Nick Blick ran into the back and hid.

Uncle Pirate looked confused.

"What should I do, Nevvy?" he asked me.

"We'd better talk to Mr. Blick," I said.

We found him on top of a pile of coffee boxes.

"This is terrible," he said. "Oh, Bob. Why did you have to be so good at your job?"

"I be sorry, Captain," Bob said.

"It's not your fault," Nick Blick said. "If this were my store, I'd pay you anything to stay. But I work for Stircrock's. Everything has to be done their way."

"But everyone likes my uncle's drinks better," I said.

Nick Blick nodded sadly.

"No one will ever come here again," he said. "I might as well quit."

"Take heart, Captain," Uncle Pirate said. "I'll learn to reef sail proper if you'll let me stay."

"Forget it," Nick Blick said. "I've always wanted

to ride my bike across the country. I suppose I might as well start. Turn out the lights when you go."

"Arh," Uncle Pirate said in a quiet voice.

We stayed until all the customers had gone away sadly. Then we went home.

Mom and Dad were waiting for us at the door.

"Where were you? It's almost ten p.m.," Mom said.

"It is?" I said.

We'd been so busy I'd never noticed.

"We was working," Uncle Pirate said. "Nevvy's got me two jobs so far."

"Working? Wilson is supposed to be in school," Dad said.

Captain Jack came out of the refrigerator.

"Have you got any homework?" he asked.

"I wasn't in school very long today," I explained. "I got sent home."

"Why? And where are your glasses?" Mom said.

"Broke them," I said. "Another fight."

"Why does a penguin care about homework?" Mom asked.

"I want to go to school," Captain Jack said. "Wilson said you'd sign me up tomorrow."

"You did?" Dad asked.

"Yes," I said.

Mom and Dad gave each other a look. I didn't think it was a good look, for Uncle Pirate or Captain Jack or me.

"And there's another thing," Dad said. "Someone has cut down all our bushes. Do you know anything about it?"

"That were me," Uncle Pirate said.

"Why?" Mom said.

"That were me first job," Uncle Pirate said. "But I weren't no good at it. Now, me second job went fine till I lost it."

"Dad, I'm afraid your coffee place is out of business," I said.

"Oh, no," Dad said.

"Can I go to school?" Captain Jack asked.

"Bed. Now. Everybody," Dad said. "I'll sort this out in the morning."

Uncle Pirate and I went up to bed.

I lay in the hammock feeling rotten.

"Nevvy, ye never told me why ye came home early today," Uncle Pirate said in the dark.

I told him about Carla Canova and the Pixi Trix trick Jason had played on me. Then I told him all about Very Elementary.

"That don't sound like no fit school for a school," Uncle Pirate said.

"That's what I tried to tell Captain Jack," I said. "You can't let him go there."

"I promised him, Nevvy," Uncle Pirate said. "I said if I was ever rescued, I'd put him in school. I were afraid he'd leave me if I didn't."

The door opened. It was Captain Jack.

"Am I going to school tomorrow or not?" he said.

"All three of us be going to school tomorrow, Captain Jack," Uncle Pirate said.

"All right, then," Captain Jack said. He went back downstairs.

"A bad school it may be," Uncle Pirate said. "But it be the only sail in sight. Good night, Nevvy."

Uncle Pirate Comes Aboard

The next day Uncle Pirate made breakfast again. Then he told Mom and Dad that I was taking him to school for show-and-tell.

"We means to be educational," he said. "Me and Captain Jack."

"Listen, Bob, when you get home, we need to talk," Dad said.

"We were up late last night, and we decided some things," Mom said.

"Arh," Uncle Pirate said. "We needs to parlay, all right. About Nevvy's school."

"We need to talk about a lot of things," Dad said.

I was sure he meant that Uncle Pirate had to leave. But where could he go?

"No," I sort of gulped. But no one heard me.

"Come, Nevvy. Come, Captain Jack," Uncle Pirate said. "Let's weigh anchor."

Captain Jack walked between us, and we each held one flipper.

"I'm so excited," he said. "I've been wanting to go to school ever since I learned to talk."

"Don't get your hopes up," I said.

Captain Jack couldn't walk very fast. It made us a little late.

When we reached school, Uncle Pirate went to the office.

"Permission to come aboard!" he shouted, and tried the door.

It was locked, of course.

"This hatch be battened," he said to me.

"You have to give the secretary food," I said. "Otherwise she won't let you in."

"Arh," Uncle Pirate said. "Never mind. We'll hail this vessel later. Where be your classroom?"

I took him to Ms. Twissel's class. It was pretty much normal. Kids were hitting each other with their

backpacks. They were stuffing each other into the closet. They were sitting on each other's heads.

Ms. Twissel was in her corner, asking if anyone would like to do a little work today. Nobody answered her.

I came in with Uncle Pirate and Captain Jack. The three of us stood together by the door.

"This is terrible," Captain Jack said. "How can I learn anything in a place like this?"

"Mollymockery," Uncle Pirate growled. "Worst I've ever seen."

Slowly everybody realized that there was a pirate with a penguin in the room. They stopped fighting and screaming and stared.

"Ms. Twissel, this is my uncle," I said. "He brought his penguin for show-and-tell."

"Permission to come aboard," Uncle Pirate said.

Ms. Twissel always looked frightened. Now she looked more frightened than usual.

"That looks like a pirate," she said.

"Arh," Uncle Pirate said. "Captain Desperate Evil Wicked Bob, former skipper of the *Hyena of the Seas*, at your service."

"Oh, no," Ms. Twissel said. "You children are bad enough. But I won't have pirates in my class. They make people walk the plank. I quit. Good-bye."

She ran out of the room.

The last we saw, she was dashing across the playground. She took off her shoes so she could run faster.

All the kids cheered and jumped up and down. They threw their books at the ceiling and clapped their hands. It was the worst we'd ever been.

"This is not what I was hoping for," said Captain Jack. "In fact, I'm scared."

The kids were screeching louder and louder. Big kids started ganging up on little ones. The little ones started to cry.

"BELAAAAAY!"

BELAAAAAAY

None of us had ever heard anything like that sound before. It sounded like it started underground and went all the way up to the stars. It shook the windows and made the door rattle. I think it dimmed the lights.

Everyone stopped what they were doing.

Uncle Pirate stomped to the front of the room. Captain Jack followed him. I stayed where I was, by the door.

Uncle Pirate looked us all up and down.

"Mollymockery," he finally said. "Which of you scurvy mop buckets knows that word?"

Nobody did.

Uncle Pirate wrote it on the board.

"It means 'the drunken rioting of sailors on Greenland whalers,'" he said. "There be nothing lower on Earth or at sea than a Greenland whaler."

He scowled at us and went on.

"Ye be the worst crew I ever saw. There be not one of ye, except my nevvy, fit to sail with me. Would I take such sculpins to the Spanish Main? The Strait of Malacca? I would not. Now, my name be Bob. Desperate Evil Wicked Bob. And unless your teacher comes back, I be captain here. Unless there's one of you flounder faces who wants to fight me for it."

There wasn't.

"Right, then," Uncle Pirate said. "What be the name of this craft, Nevvy?"

"It doesn't have a name," I said. "It's just a classroom. Room four."

"It be a craft now," Uncle Pirate said. "I names her the *Kraken*. Who says different?"

Nobody said anything.

"Who knows what a kraken be?" Uncle Pirate asked.

No one did.

"It be the giant squid," he said. "A fearsome beast. From now on this be our ship, and ye be her crew. A crew be all one gang. They works together and they doesn't fight. And they never sinks to mollymockery."

"You're not a real pirate," Scott said. "There aren't any

real pirates anymore. You're not a real pirate, and I don't have to do what you say."

Captain Jack walked over to where Scott was standing.

"I suppose there's no such thing as a talking penguin, either," he said.

Scott's mouth dropped open. So did everyone else's.

"You follow your orders," Captain Jack said. "Or I'll peck you so hard you won't sit down for the rest of your life."

"Okay," Scott said.

"Now, Captain Jack came to this school to learn," Uncle Pirate said. "He wants to know what ye know. Ye must help him. First, get this deck shipshape and Bristol fashion."

"That means clean everything up," I said.

So we got to work. It didn't take long until the room was clean and neat. Then we all sat down in our assigned seats.

Uncle Pirate nodded.

"Now, who be Carla Canova?" he said.

Carla stood up. I thought she was bigger than she'd been yesterday.

"That's me," she said.

"Ye look to me like a right proper first mate," Uncle Pirate said. "Be ye willing to lead this crew when I be elsewhere?"

"I be," she said.

"Then, take this," Uncle Pirate said.

He gave Carla a little silver whistle. I'd never seen one like it before.

"Blow like this," he said.

He showed her how to blow three high notes.

"When ye swabs hear this whistle, ye drop everything and run to it," Uncle Pirate said. "It means there's orders. Understood?"

"Say 'Aye, aye' when he talks like that," Captain Jack told everyone.

"Aye, aye," we all said.

"Right. Now ye must all have pirate names," Uncle Pirate said. "First Mate Carla be tall, so she be Long Carla."

He pointed at Scott. "You, ye lubber, what be your name?"

"Scott Jenkins."

"Ye have sandy hair," Uncle Pirate said. "Ye be Sand Crab Scott from now on."

He went up and down the rows learning our names and telling us new ones. When he was done with everyone else, he came over to me.

"And ye be Binnacle Will," he said.

"Why?" I asked.

"Because the binnacle be where we keeps the compass," Uncle Pirate said. "And Nevvy, ye never steers me wrong."

"Arh," I said.

"Now Captain Jack wants to learn something," Uncle Pirate said. "What would ye like to know first, Captain Jack?"

"I want to learn to read."

"Long Carla, go in yon corner and teach Captain Jack," Uncle Pirate said.

"I won't do it," she said.

"Why not?" Uncle Pirate asked.

"I'm not good at reading," she said. "I'm a year behind."

"Ye be perfect, then," Uncle Pirate said. "Captain Jack don't know nothing at all."

"Do you know the alphabet?" Captain Jack asked her.

Carla said, "The whole thing."

"Show me how it works," Captain Jack said.

Carla took his flipper, and they went into the corner and got busy.

"Can I teach him arithmetic?" Jason asked.

"Can I teach him science?" Scott asked.

"I reckon ye all have something to teach Captain Jack," Uncle Pirate said. "But now ye must stand by to sign articles. Where be a big piece of paper?"

I got a poster board and a black marker for him.

Uncle Pirate wrote slowly. He kept muttering to himself.

When he was finished, he said, "Any swab who hopes to serve with me and Captain Jack, make your marks now."

He held up the poster board. It said:

1) We be the crew of the good ship Kraken. We swears to stand together in all storms, battles, and other pirate dangers.

2) We swears to follow all lawful orders shipshape and Bristol fashion.

3) We also swears never to mutiny.

4) Captain Desperate Evil Wicked Bob swears never to hang, shoot, or keelhaul any member of the crew.

5) Except for mutiny.

6) All treasure is to be divided up even.

7) We be the crew of the good ship Kraken. We swears to stand together in all storms, battles, and other pirate dangers. We swears it again.

"What about the penguin?" everyone asked.

"Arh," Uncle Pirate said. He wrote:

8) Captain Desperate Evil Wicked Bob swears to bring Captain Jack to school every day. Unless the bird be sick.

"Now sign, ye slimy elvers," Uncle Pirate said. "Sign, or go ashore."

We all signed our pirate names. No one wanted to miss going to school with Captain Jack.

The bell rang.

"What be that?" Uncle Pirate said. "Be the enemy in view? Be there a sail on the horizon?"

"That's recess," we said.

"Clear decks for recess!" Uncle Pirate roared.

Uncle Pirate's Song

Captain Jack didn't want to go out for recess.

"I just started learning," he said to Long Carla. "Please, let's keep working."

So they did, and the rest of us went out.

That recess was different. No one in my class hit anyone else. No one was mean. We played tag and called each other by our pirate names. Other kids wondered why we weren't killing each other like they were.

Just before the bell rang, Uncle Pirate came out on the playground. He had Captain Jack on one side and Carla on the other.

Carla blew on her whistle. We all stopped playing and came running.

"Smartly done," Uncle Pirate told us. "Now, here be your orders: Form ranks and march to your deck. Ship's company—attention!"

We made one line behind Carla and one behind Captain Jack. Back we went to class while everyone stared at us.

"Who's that?" they asked.

"Our new teacher," we told them.

"Is he really a pirate?" they asked.

"We're all pirates," we said. "Arh."

Uncle Pirate taught us long division next. He'd make one of us read a problem. The problem would say something like "If Mary has ten apples and gives away six to Mike and Bill, how many does each have if they all have an equal number, and what is the remainder?"

"Belay that," Uncle Pirate would growl. Then he'd say, "Say I steals three hundred fifty-two pieces of eight. Then Rotten Ralph and One-Eared Phil claims equal shares of the loot. How much does they get, and what does I keep? And how does we decide who gets the extra bit without a fight?"

It made it a lot more interesting.

〰〰〰〰

All that morning kids and teachers kept coming by. The kids wanted to see the pirate and penguin. The teachers wanted to know why our room was so quiet.

At lunch we all sat together. We called each other by

our pirate names. We shared things to eat. The other classes just stared at us. Then Long Carla blew her whistle, and we all lined up and went back to our classroom together.

It was just after lunch when Ms. Quern peeked around the door.

"There's a rumor that this room is being quiet," she said. "What's wrong with this class? Why isn't it noisy and awful? Why aren't you hitting each other?"

Uncle Pirate stared at Ms. Quern. Then he pointed at Long Carla.

"First Mate, who be yon handsome female?" he asked.

"That's Ms. Quern, the principal's secretary," Carla said.

"Welcome aboard, ma'am," Uncle Pirate said, and saluted. "I be Captain Desperate Evil Wicked Bob, at your service."

Ms. Quern looked startled.

Then Uncle Pirate said, "Ma'am, I have taken command of this crew, and my penguin be learning his letters. I thought nothing could make this day finer. But ye have brightened it like a whole chest of doubloons. Thank ye for coming aboard."

Ms. Quern did something very strange. Something no one had ever seen her do before. She smiled. It was a nice smile.

"Why, thank you," she said. "Are you really a pirate?"

"We all be pirates on this deck, ma'am," Uncle Pirate said. "All articled and proper."

"And is that a real penguin?"

"Yes it is," said Captain Jack.

Ms. Quern went over and softly petted Captain Jack's head. He made a little sort of purring sound.

"What a wonderful penguin," she said.

"Captain Jack don't let just anyone pet him, ma'am," Uncle Pirate said. "Ye must be a special fine lady as well as a handsome one."

"You know," Ms. Quern said. "I've always thought pirates were very romantic."

"And there's many a pirate thinks secretaries be romantic too," Uncle Pirate said.

"Really?" said Ms. Quern, smiling more. "I never heard that."

"Oh, there be many a song sung by a lonely pirate under a tropical moon about some secretary loved and lost," Uncle Pirate said. "Would ye care to hear one?"

"Oh, no," Ms. Quern said. "I couldn't. Never. No. Thank you, but no."

"I knows all the verses," Uncle Pirate said.

Ms. Quern's cheeks turned all pink.

"No. I must go back to the office," she said.

"Arh!" said Uncle Pirate.

And Ms. Quern went out of the room, almost skipping.

We could hardly believe that Ms. Quern liked Uncle Pirate. She didn't like anybody. But then again, who wouldn't like Uncle Pirate?

At afternoon recess everyone asked Captain Jack to come to their room the next day.

"I'll come if it's quiet," he said. "I can't learn when there's mollymockery."

"We promise," the kids from the other classes said. "Whatever it is, we won't do it."

For the rest of the afternoon Captain Jack wrote the

alphabet over and over. He held a pencil in his beak while Carla watched.

When the last bell rang, he said, "Thank you, Long Carla. You're smart. Tomorrow I want to learn to read."

"Okay," Carla said. "We'll try."

Right at three o'clock Uncle Pirate brought me and Captain Jack to the office door. It was locked.

"Take me hands, shipmates," he said. "I needs courage."

So I took one hand and Captain Jack gave him his flipper. Uncle Pirate threw back his shoulders and sang at the door.

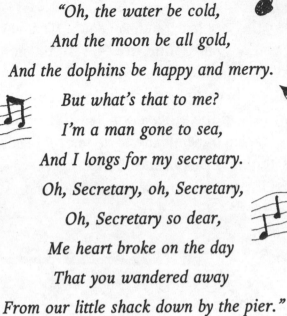

"Oh, the water be cold,
And the moon be all gold,
And the dolphins be happy and merry.
But what's that to me?
I'm a man gone to sea,
And I longs for my secretary.
Oh, Secretary, oh, Secretary,
Oh, Secretary so dear,
Me heart broke on the day
That you wandered away
From our little shack down by the pier."

The song had a lot of verses. By the time it was over, Uncle Pirate had tears in his eyes. We waited there for a few minutes, but the door didn't open. Finally Uncle Pirate said, "Come, shipmates. It be time to weigh anchor."

When we were outside, he said quietly, "Nevvy, that be the finest-looking woman I've seen since the figure-head on the good old *Hyena of the Seas*."

74

When we got home from school, Mom and Dad were waiting.

"Bob, it's time we had that talk," Dad said.

Before he could say any more, I said, "Guess what? Uncle Pirate's my new teacher."

"What?" Dad said.

"What happened to Ms. Twissel?" Mom asked.

"She left when we came," Captain Jack said.

"Uncle Pirate and Captain Jack made everybody stop fighting," I said. "He's the best teacher we have. And all the other kids want Captain Jack to visit their rooms."

"Bob, that's wonderful," Mom said.

"I have homework," Captain Jack said. "Spelling the alphabet. It goes ABCDEFGHIJKLMNOPQRSTUVW XYZ. I like homework."

"Now, Steve, what was ye wanting to parlay about?" Uncle Pirate asked.

"I'm not sure now," Dad said. "You really have a teaching job?"

"Arh," Uncle Pirate said.

"Well, then?" Dad said to Mom.

"Well, it's still very crowded," Mom said.

"But Uncle Pirate's got a job now. When they pay him, he can help buy food and stuff."

"I could buy glasses for Nevvy," Uncle Pirate said.

75

"That will be a big help," Dad said.

"All right, Bob," Mom said. "You and Captain Jack can stay, I guess."

"Of course I can stay, Emmy," Uncle Pirate said. "I'd not leave ye, and Steve, and Nevvy. And Captain Jack be happy here."

"ABCDEFGHIJKLMNOP," Captain Jack said. "Tomorrow I'm going to learn to read."

I was so scared I was almost shaking. Uncle Pirate really thought he had a job. But I'd told a lie, or close to it. I knew he had to sign papers or something to get paid. What would Principal Purvis do when he finally realized he had a pirate in his school?

Mom and Dad looked around at the crowded little condo.

"Arh," they both said.

Commodore Purvis

Everything was different at Very Elementary the next day. All the kids were waiting to see what would happen next. They were all behaving and staying quiet. That lasted for almost an hour.

Then we heard a terrible noise coming from the sixth grade. We always heard terrible noises coming from the sixth grade, so we didn't pay much attention. But then the teacher, Ms. Mipps, came running down the hall to our room.

"Captain, my sixth graders are coming," she said. "Run for your life."

"All hands stand by to repel boarders," Uncle Pirate said. "But first let's give them a chance to parlay."

He went and stood in the door. Captain Jack went over and stood behind him. So did I. Carla got the kids lined up behind her. Ms. Mipps's class didn't know what they were up against.

All the sixth graders crowded in front of Uncle Pirate. "What do ye want, ye chum buckets?" he said.

"We want to be pirates too," they said. "Come and teach our class."

Ms. Mipps was standing in the corner that Ms. Twissel always used to use.

"Captain, will it suit ye for me to deal with these mutinous dogs?" Uncle Pirate asked her.

"Yes, please," she said.

"Long Carla to the quarterdeck," Uncle Pirate said. "Take over the ship."

"Everybody take your seats," Long Carla said. "Ms. Mipps, start teaching."

So we did, and Ms. Mipps did.

We were all quiet for Ms. Mipps. Captain Jack started learning addition from Scott. But everyone was waiting for Uncle Pirate to come back.

Recess came, but the sixth grade didn't come out for it. The rest of us just stood around listening. Every kid in every class was wondering what Uncle Pirate was doing to the sixth graders. When recess was over, we went back in. There was still no sound from the sixth grade.

Lunchtime came. We made our two lines and followed Carla and Captain Jack to the lunchroom. All the other kids went there in a crowd around us, trying to get close to Captain Jack.

Then, when we were all sitting down with our trays, into the lunchroom marched the sixth grade.

They followed Uncle Pirate over to our tables.

"Shipmates, on your feet," he ordered.

We all stood up.

"Crew of the *Kraken*, I give you the crew of the good ship *Sea Dragon*. They has all signed articles. They means to sail a true course from now on. No mollymockery and no mutiny. Captain Mipps, I gives you back your crew."

One of the boys stepped forward.

"I be your first mate, Captain," he said. "My name be Octopus Charlie."

"But I can't be a pirate," Ms. Mipps said. "I don't know how."

"Ye can all learn together," Uncle Pirate said. "Captain Jack!"

"What?" Captain Jack said.

"Take the afternoon watch aboard the *Sea Dragon*," Uncle Pirate said. "They has a lesson on Antarctica today. Ye can help Captain Mipps teach it."

"Aye, aye," Captain Jack said.

The sixth graders all sat down with us. We told each other our pirate names. We called each other matey. All of them told me how neat I was to have an uncle like Uncle Pirate.

Just before lunch was over, a kid from kindergarten came up to Uncle Pirate.

"Can we be pirates?" he asked.

"We all want to be pirates!" the kids started to shout.

But they got quiet as soon as Uncle Pirate stood up.

"Vote," he said. "Who sails with Desperate Evil Wicked Bob? Who sails with Captain Jack?"

Every hand went up. Every hand, even the teachers'. Even the ladies who worked in the lunchroom voted.

"Who stays ashore?" Uncle Pirate asked.

No one voted for that.

"I'll be comin' aboard to sign ye to articles," Uncle Pirate said. "Meantime, keep all shipshape and Bristol fashion. And no mollymockery."

The bell rang. The sixth graders got up and marched out of the lunchroom. Captain Jack went with them.

That afternoon Uncle Pirate named all the other classrooms. He named the kindergarten the *Swordfish*. The first grade was the *Stingray*. The second grade was the *Narwhal*. The third grade was the *Sea Lion*, and the fifth grade was the *Hammerhead*. He gave all the kids their pirate names and signed them to articles.

By afternoon recess every kid and teacher aboard Very Elementary School was a pirate.

After recess Principal Purvis came to the door.

"What's going on?" he asked.

"Who be ye, ye slimy sack of tuna guts?" Uncle Pirate asked.

"That's Principal Purvis," I said.

"Welcome aboard, Commodore," Uncle Pirate said, and saluted.

"My secretary's wearing a bandanna and an eye patch," Principal Purvis said.

"When I asked her why, she told me to come down to the fourth grade and find out."

"This is the good ship *Kraken*," Carla said. "That's our captain."

"Arh," Uncle Pirate said.

"What happened to Ms. Twissel?" Principal Purvis asked.

"She ran away," we all said.

"That's awful," said Mr. Purvis. "Now who can I get to teach this class?"

"Captain Desperate Evil Wicked Bob," we all said.

"Is that you?" Mr. Purvis asked.

"Aye, aye," Uncle Pirate said.

"Are you a teacher?" Principal Purvis said.

"I taught that penguin to talk," Uncle Pirate said.

"Yes, he did," said Captain Jack.

"You can't just go around teaching things," Principal Purvis said. "You need a certificate."

"I has a certificate as a ship's captain," Uncle Pirate said.

"You look like a pirate," Principal Purvis said.

"I were a pirate," Uncle Pirate said.

Principal Purvis's eyes lit up.

"Have you got any buried treasure?" he asked.

"No, Commodore, I has not," Uncle Pirate said.

"Too bad," Principal Purvis said.

83

Then he said, "Are those pistols real?"

"Arh," Uncle Pirate said.

Principal Purvis came closer to Uncle Pirate. "Can I see one?"

Uncle Pirate handed over a pistol. Principal Purvis started rubbing it like he was petting a cat. He kept touching the little skull on the hammer.

"Where did you get these?" Principal Purvis asked.

"They were give me by my dear friend No-Good Creepy Mike," Uncle Pirate said. "When I were but a little pirate."

"Where did he get them?" Principal Purvis asked.

"He never said," Uncle Pirate answered. "I reckon he stole them, being a pirate."

"You can't have guns on school grounds," said Principal Purvis. "You'd better give them to me for safekeeping."

Uncle Pirate handed over the other pistol.

"Do you want me cutlass, too, Commodore?" Uncle Pirate said.

"No, no," said Principal Purvis.

"There's no rule against cutlasses. Keep it. I don't care."

He smiled and stuffed the pistols into his belt. I thought they looked awful there. His smile looked awful too. It wasn't like Ms. Quern's.

"All right," Principal Purvis said. "You're hired. I'll be under my desk if you need anything."

"Aye, aye, Commodore," Uncle Pirate said, and saluted again.

Principal Purvis went away.

We all cheered.

Captain Jack came back from the sixth grade, which was now the *Sea Dragon*, and sat next to me.

"I told them about Antarctica, and they told me about the moon," he said. "I learned a lot. This is a good school."

I looked around the room, where all us pirates were quiet and happy, and everything was shipshape and Bristol fashion.

"It sure is," I said.

Jolly Rogers

The next day two things happened. The first was in the morning. Ms. Quern brought Uncle Pirate a big black flag with the skull and crossbones on it. Just like Principal Purvis had said, she was wearing a bandanna and a big black eye patch.

Uncle Pirate grinned when he saw her.

"Ma'am, ye look finer with one eye than Anne Bonney or Grania O'Malley ever looked with two apiece," he said.

"I've made one of these for every room," Ms. Quern said. "I think you call it the Jolly Roger."

"Ms. Quern, ye are a canny hand," Uncle Pirate said. "The Jolly Roger be the one thing we needed."

He put it up next to the American flag.

"Now, mateys, stand and pledge your oath," he said.

We said the Pledge the way we always did it.

"We pledge allegiance to the Untied Snakes of America and to all that other stuff we don't understand. Amen."

"Nay, ye sculpins," Uncle Pirate said. "Like this: Though we be pirates, we still pledges allegiance to the flag of the United States of America, which we loves like we loves the Jolly Roger."

So we all did it again, and that was that.

"That was so beautiful," Ms. Quern said. "Did you write it?"

"Nay," Uncle Pirate said. "That were just what Captain Jean Laffite and his men said when they went into battle at New Orleans, fighting for Andy Jackson. It be Laffite's Oath."

"Laffite's Oath," said Ms. Quern. "It's so strong. So noble. Do you think I could be a pirate too?"

"Ma'am, I never saw a woman more likely to come up through the hawsehole than ye," Uncle Pirate said.

"That means yes," said Captain Jack.

So Ms. Quern signed articles. She blushed when she did it. Uncle Pirate took her papers and put them next to his heart.

"But I need a pirate name," Ms. Quern said.

"What be your first name, ma'am?" Uncle Pirate said softly.

"Eunice," Ms. Quern said.

Uncle Pirate said, "I names ye Ferocious Lovely Eunice."

"Oh," Ms. Quern said. "Oh."

And she put both of her hands to her cheeks and went out of the room.

"A canny, canny hand," Uncle Pirate said.

The other thing happened in the afternoon. It was just before the end of the day. All of a sudden the intercom came on in every room. It was Ms. Quern's voice:

"All hands on deck! Stand by to repel boarders. To

the principal's office now. Shake a leg, ye scurvy dogs!"

"Long Carla, blow to battle stations," Uncle Pirate said. "Crew of the *Kraken*, follow me."

We hurried down the hall. All around us the other crews were coming behind their captains. When we got to the principal's office, we saw a man in a very nice suit running away. Ms. Quern was chasing him and throwing books.

"Drop those pistols, you horrible son of a squid," she shouted.

She hit him right in the back of the head with *How to Retire Early.*

"That man has Captain Desperate Evil Wicked Bob's pistols," she told us. "Overhaul him."

The man looked back over his shoulder and saw every kid in the school coming after him. So were the teachers,

89

the lunchroom ladies, the janitors, and Captain Jack.

"Help," he said, and threw down the pistols.

Ms. Quern picked them up and handed them to Uncle Pirate.

"What means all this, shipmate?" Uncle Pirate asked.

"That man came into the office and asked for Principal Purvis," she said. "I recognized him. He's on *Attic Antics* on television. It's a show where people bring in their antiques, and he tells them what they're worth. He went in and saw the principal. Mr. Purvis closed the door, which he never does, so of course I listened. I heard 'pistols,' 'unique find,' and 'one million dollars.' Then he came out with the pistols, and Mr. Purvis said, 'Ms. Quern, I'm retiring. Take over.' That's when I rang the alarm."

"Where be Purvis?" Uncle Pirate said.

"Look," said Scott. "He's getting away."

Principal Purvis had sneaked out the window of Ms. Quern's office and was running for his car.

"Captain, permission to charge," Long Carla said.

"Long Carla, pick me up," Captain Jack said. "Please."

"CHARGE!" Uncle Pirate roared.

We did. The sixth graders charged. The fifth graders charged. The fourth graders charged. The third graders, second graders, first graders, and kindergartners all charged, and the janitors and lunchroom ladies and teachers charged with us.

But the fastest of us all was Long Carla, even though she was carrying Captain Jack.

And Captain Jack was flapping his flippers and squawking and shouting, "Faster, Long Carla, faster."

Principal Purvis made it to his car. He pulled out his keys. But he was so scared that he hit the wrong button, and instead of unlocking the doors, he set off the car alarm. That scared him more, and he dropped the keys. He bent over to pick them up, and Long Carla threw Captain Jack at him. Captain Jack landed on top of Principal Purvis and started to peck him all over.

"No, no, stop, please," begged Principal Purvis.

He lay on the asphalt and put his arms over his head.

But Captain Jack didn't stop until we all had Principal Purvis surrounded.

"Now, what means this slipping anchor, Commodore?" Uncle Pirate said.

Principal Purvis picked himself up.

"That really hurts," he said.

"Start talking," said Captain Jack. "Or you'll find out what really hurts."

"Explain yourself, sir," Uncle Pirate said.

"I hate this place," Principal Purvis said. "So I spend all my time under my desk. When I'm down there, I read about how to make a lot of money without working, so I can retire early. One of the things I read about is treasure. Did you ever hear of the fight between Captain Stinking Nasty Adams and Captain Foul Play Jenkins?"

"Arh," Uncle Pirate said. "That were a famous fight. All pirates know of it."

"Well, one of the books I read said that Captain Adams shot Captain Jenkins with two pistols just like yours. It said they were the only ones like them in the world, and no one knew what had happened to them. I knew I had a fortune if I could just get them away from you. So I did."

"What shall we do with this treacherous squalus?" Ms. Quern said.

"Hang him!" shouted the sixth graders.

"Keelhaul him!" shouted the fifth graders.

"Make him walk the plank!" shouted the fourth graders.

"Maroon him!" shouted the third graders.

"Clap him in irons!" shouted the second graders.

"Put him in the brig!" shouted the first graders.

"Make him stay in at recess," shouted the kindergartners.

"Make him go to the office," said one little kid.

"Young squid, ye've a good head on your shoulders," Uncle Pirate said. "The office be the very place we need. Purvis and I must parlay."

He turned to us.

"We needs a committee of respectable pirates to tell

all crews the results of our parlay. Who will ye vote for?"

We elected Ms. Quern, Captain Jack, Long Carla, and me.

Then the six of us went to the office.

"That were not very nice, Commodore," Uncle Pirate said when we were all sitting except Captain Jack.

"Well, everything was awful here, and then you came along and made it all fun and happy," said Principal Purvis. "And everyone else got to be a pirate but me. That wasn't very nice either."

The committee booed Principal Purvis, but Uncle Pirate said, "Commodore, ye be the commodore. That means ye be commander of this whole squadron. Didn't ye know that?"

"I am?" Principal Purvis said.

"Arh," Uncle Pirate said.

"Don't let him be one of us," Ms. Quern shouted, and everyone agreed with her.

But Uncle Pirate said, "Nay, shipmates. For this man has acted more like a pirate than any one of us since I came aboard. Low-down and sneaky and greedy for loot. This swab has the heart and soul of a pirate."

"I do?" said Principal Purvis. "Maybe that's why I've never liked being a principal."

"Mayhap," Uncle Pirate said. "But a pirate must live by

the code of the pirates. And if ye signs on to cruise with us, ye must be true and faithful to all, and steer clear of mollymockery. Will ye sign articles, Purvis?"

"Sure," said Principal Purvis. "But I want a pirate name."

"Ye be Sneaky Low-Down Backstabbing Purvis," Uncle Pirate said.

"Sneaky Low-Down Backstabbing Purvis? That's wonderful," Principal Purvis said. "Thank you, Captain."

"Arh," Uncle Pirate said.

So Ms. Quern typed up some articles, and Mr. Purvis signed them. Then he gave Uncle Pirate the check for one million dollars that the man from the television show had given him.

Uncle Pirate tore it up.

"Ye be one of us now, Purvis," he said. "We be ready to serve under you and obey all lawful orders. But if ye ever tries anything like this again, I'll give ye to Captain Jack."

"Aye, aye, Captain," said Sneaky Purvis.

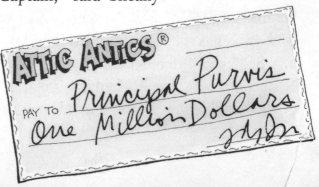

A Right Good Crew

Uncle Pirate sold the pistols to a museum. With part of the money he bought a big house, close to Ms. Quern. Now we all live with him. There are rooms for Mom and Dad, Uncle Pirate, and me. Captain Jack has his own refrigerator now.

Every morning the three of us walk to school. It has a new name now. Jolly Roger Elementary. We all say Laffite's Oath every morning. The lunchroom serves thunder slump every Tuesday.

Ms. Twissel took over Stircrock's. Uncle Pirate went there and showed her how to make his special drinks. She renamed it Ms. Twissel's Desperate Evil Wicked Coffees. Nick Blick came back from his trip and went to work for her. She gives him lots of days off to ride his bike.

Captain Jack has learned so much he'll be in fifth grade with me next year. He goes to the library with

Long Carla after school. She reads a lot better than she did because she has to keep ahead of Captain Jack.

"That Long Carla is really smart," Captain Jack says every day.

Everything's shipshape and Bristol fashion. But sometimes Uncle Pirate gazes off across the playground and looks sad. Just for a minute. It's like he's watching for something. A sail, maybe.

"Uncle Pirate, do you ever miss having a real ship?" I asked him yesterday.

"Sometimes, Nevvy, I does," he said. "I sees a seagull high overhead, or the tall clouds sailing by like fat merchantmen waiting to be plucked. Then I longs for the feel of a deck under my feet and the bite of a fierce sea wind. But then I thinks, 'It be the crew that makes the ship.' And Nevvy, we be a right good crew."

"Arh," I said.

· GLOSSARY ·

Avast: Literally, "hold fast."

Bilges: The lowest, and smelliest, part of a ship, between the lowest deck and the hull.

Carronades: Large but light cannons made of brass.

Commodore: Usually a courtesy title for anyone in command of more than one ship.

Davy Jones: The king of the undersea world.

Elvers: Young eels.

Foc's'le: Literally, "fore castle." The sleeping quarters in the forward part of the ship.

Hawsehole: A hole in a ship through which a cable—a hawser—passes. To "come up through the hawsehole" is to be promoted to officer's rank.

Kraken: Norwegian name for the giant squid.

Lubber: Someone clumsy and not very bright. Not an ideal shipmate.

Mollymockery: The term really does mean what Uncle Pirate says it does. A mollymock is any one of several large species of seabirds.

Razee: To cut down a ship by one or more decks.

Sea Cook: At sea, the cook ranks below everyone else.

Sea-doggin': The original sea dogs were the English sailors of the sixteenth century who fought against Spain.

Squalus: The Latin word for shark. Rare in English.

· The Secretary Song ·

Oh, the water be cold,
And the moon be all gold,
And the dolphins be happy and merry.
But what's that to me?
I'm a man gone to sea,
And I longs for my secretary.
Oh, Secretary, oh, Secretary,
Oh, Secretary so dear,
Me heart broke on the day
That you wandered away
From our little shack down by the pier.